STORY 106

106 stories of 106 words
from the 2011 Competition

Two Lochs Radio with **Gairloch Writers' Group**

illustrated by

Viveca Port (Adult Section)
Ruairdhri Wright (12-17 Section)
pupils of **Kinlochewe Primary School** (11 & Under Section)

Stories and illustrations © the individually named authors
Compilation © 2012 Wester Ross Radio Ltd

First published 2012 by
Wester Ross Radio Ltd ("Two Lochs Radio") and the Gairloch Writers' Group
Harbour Centre, Pier Road, Gairloch, IV21 2BQ

All rights reserved

Wester Ross Radio Ltd has asserted its right to be identified as author of this compilation and the individual contributors have asserted their rights to be identified as authors of their respective contributions.

Cover image photography and Design by Jeremy Fenton

Print by Wordworks Ltd, Gairloch

ISBN 978-0-9564657-1-9

Carol,
"Our" 106 story began Saturday 24th March 2018. And from August the same year S.B.'s & S.R.V.'s have never been the same since! Thank you for being my radio buddy.
G x

December 2019

The Story 106 Competition

Two Lochs Radio is the smallest licensed radio station in the UK. It operates on a not-for-profit basis, and its programmes are all presented by volunteers. The station broadcasts locally on 106 and 106.6 FM, and on the Internet at www.2LR.co.uk.

When a competition for short stories of 106 words was suggested, both the radio and the local writers' group welcomed the idea. Four local residents volunteered to be judges and two generous sponsors came forward so that prizes could be awarded. The competition was announced through many radio broadcasts and in the local paper, the *Gairloch & District Times*, and the organisers awaited the entries.

The response was overwhelming, with over 200 entries in the three categories (adult, 12 to 17 years, and 11 years and under). The prize winners were announced and their stories were read out at the Two Lochs Radio AGM in November 2011. But there were many more great stories that deserved recognition.

Therefore it was decided to produce a small book of a selected 106 stories, thus keeping the number theme, as a tribute to those who entered the competition and as entertainment for you, the reader. It was difficult to choose the entries, and the booklet production team would like to thank everyone who sent in stories and who helped to make the competition such a success. Apart from the printing, all the work has been voluntary; any profits will go into a fund for a future competition, which we hope will be equally successful.

Adult Section

Stories are in alphabetical order of title, except the prize winners which come first.

Kirsty Adam	*In Small Time*
Barbara Allen	*New Start, Heart of Stone, Job Done, The Nobody Faces*
P.M. Angier	*"Him", Kevin and the Chicken*
John Beck	*Storm Damage*
Hilary Brown	*The Escape*
Mark Cooper	*Myth & Magic in Melvaig, The Blue Men*
Jeremy Fenton	*The Dream, The Number*
Alison Grove	*Cover Story, Like the Back of your Hand*
René Grun	*Behind Every Successful Man, Buy Garlic Today, New World, Withdrawal*
Gillian Holt	*Nobody's Dog*
Katy Leitch	*Seeing the Light*
Tom Lister	*A Night on the Tiles*
Christine MacIver	*Birthday Wishes*
Fiona Mackenzie	*Highland Tour*
Tracy McLachlan	*Rainbow*
Nancy MacLeod	*A Case of Murder?*
Ian MacMillan	*Testing the Waters*
Dorothy Malone	*The Bottle and the Glass, Desperate Measures, No Escape, Only Yesterday, Reunited*
R. Mapstone	*The Journey*
Serena Mason	*Lot 106, The Same Wavelength*
George Milne	*Out with a Bang, The Price of Freedom*
Patricia Moon	*The Endless War, Life's Anomalies*
Mike Northeast	*Choices*
Clare O'Brien Wright	*Amnesiacs, Ellen, New Build, The Snowglobe*
Mike Powley	*Robot, The Seedlings, Shoes and Gloves and Things, Superheron, Termination at Toothache*
Shirley Powley	*Opportune Moment, Rough Play, That Day*
Jane Rowe	*Change-over Day, Double Vision, For Dad — with Love*
Sandy	*Crofter Boy*
Paula Wild	*Dear Ernest, The Struggle to Survive*
Alasdair Wright	*Chromium Steal, The End of Murdo's Croft, Miss Quigley's Percentage, Seeing in the Dark*

FIRST PRIZE

New Start

Tomorrow I'll do something different. Not sweep leaves, wash pots, do anything I'm asked. I'll be disobedient with no civil attached.

Maybe a model, swanking down the catwalk, turning my head in opposition to my hips, strutting my stuff, turning heads.

Change the catwalk for a gangplank, I'll be a pirate. "Female pirate" I hear you laugh, "whoever heard of that!" I'll bet you've heard of Margaret Thatcher.

A woman of easy virtue, brash and controlling, or scared, walking the streets looking for a punter, maybe making some money.

I sense your fear, taste my own, university sounds dull and faraway. I want to sweep leaves.

Barbara Allen

SECOND PRIZE

Myth & Magic in Melvaig

There be goblins in Melvaig.

On pebbled beaches they disguise themselves as discarded tyres and plastic flotsam amongst boulders big as aurochs.

We scamper over the old troll bridge with high squeals and mock gravity, Flowerdale bows clutched in elven hands, to stalk goblins up tide and down dune.

"Look, a big black one!" Twang!

Goblins scattered, a bemused seal looking out across the sea's pewter deck is made mermaid. Fair folk from the rock pools build rings in the seaweed. The sky glows roseate when we trudge back, quest fulfilled.

"Daddy, a dragon" chirrups the youngest as a sea eagle soars languidly above our home.

Mark Cooper

Adult

THIRD PRIZE

Change-over Day

Change-over day — time to roam through the old house. And what a change-over! Gone the pig pen and the cow byre; gone the burning peats and the simmering crock; gone the flag floor and rush mats; gone the box beds.

She likes it though. It was so clean and bright, so light and airy. "I'd make short shrift of the housework now," she thought.

Voices outside! She took a last look and, as always, smiled at the framed writing on the wall. "1861 census — Morag Mackenzie".

As excited children burst into their holiday home, Morag Mackenzie slowly faded back into the walls of her croft house.

Jane Rowe

Amnesiacs

I don't remember who we are. Just your easy walk, your knife in your hand, the grind of bone against blade. You would have killed me sooner if I had asked you to.

Life is a dream that keeps ending in death. We wake at the wrong time. I do not know my name.

I am always shut out until the door opens and you squint into the light that engulfs me, and I remember that we roared through the world like monsters, bloody and exultant, eating everything in our path. Then I forget again, and I am nothing but an amnesiac shadow, following your ghost.

Clare O'Brien Wright

Behind Every Successful Man

"You're an idiot."
She slapped her forehead, he thought she might dent it.
"You spent money to advertise building a Jacuzzi?"
She pronounced it TSHAKKOUZZEE, spitting.
"You think people in Gairloch will get naked and sit in a tub in their yard in the rain?"
The phone rang. He picked it up.
"Hello... Yes... Alright, I'll come over. We can discuss what size Jacuzzi is best for you."
She glared.
The newspaper rustled behind him as he left.
On the way to the pub he thought of how good a friend Jim was, having phoned him as he'd promised. He'd have to stand Jim a pint, cheers.

René Grun

Birthday Wishes

At 4am on the morning of her 50th birthday Diane knew her marriage was dead, it had been for years but this time she would finally end it. There had always been various excuses in the past, "didn't want to upset the children's education, her father was ill, she couldn't afford to rent somewhere". But now at last there was nothing in her way. She would, of course, lose weight, have her hair highlighted; join the Art Group, the Book Club and take French Classes. The possibilities were endless, weren't they?

At 4am on the morning of her 60th birthday Diane knew her marriage was dead...

Christine MacIver
Commended

The Blue Men

The Blue Men came for them in their home at four.

The family slept in the grey May dawn as the clock calmly washed the bedroom with its sea-green glow. None woke to the crash of a window breaking near the foot of the stairs. Two masked, goggled monochrome beasts with guns, cordage and predatory purpose surged towards the sleepers through the darkened house. They woke, as torchlight flashed and the Blue Men stormed inside.

Minds in a maelstrom, hearts pounding they were blindfolded, tied and taunted. Only some mutual touch gave pathetic comfort.

By six, the Blue Men had torn the family apart.

Mark Cooper

The Bottle and the Glass

Each morning Pierre pushed a glass and a bottle towards the old soldier. "Cognac, monsieur." It was a statement rather than a question.

But Marcel Dupont said not a word. He drank and when finished he threw a few centimes onto the counter and left.

And this went on day after day after day.

The morning he didn't appear Pierre was concerned.

"M. Dupont est mort," a customer told him.

Pierre picked up the brandy bottle and replaced it high on the shelf. He rummaged in a drawer, found some black ribbon and tied it around the bottle's neck.

"C'est pour la belle France. Merci monsieur."

Dorothy Malone

Buy Garlic Today

Tim got bored and invented a joke about aliens, and put it on the internet.

A tall, gaunt, pale guy rang Tim's doorbell the next day.

"I can confirm your suspicions," the gaunt guy said. "We gain passage into humans by way of genetically modified foods. It's fair trade — humans get Twitter, Kindle, Starbucks, Google."

"But, that'd be almost 300 million people in America alone who're aliens."

"Yes, Tim. They're the Groups."

"Groups?"

"Group A, B, AB, and O."

"And you?"

"I'm VIP."

"Very Important Person?" Tim smirked, uneasy now, looking up.

"Vampires, Interplanetary," the guy hissed, leaned over fast, bit Tim's throat eyes wide open.

René Grun

A Case of Murder?

Seamus stretched himself out in front of the glowing fire exuding an air of contentment belying his earlier involvement in a brutal murder.

For several days he had been aware that all was not well in the farmhouse kitchen. Comments regarding his status as No. 1 mouser had been made. Evidence of unwanted visitors had been noted...

Swift action was required or demotion to the barn was a distinct possibility.

Having cased the joint, he took up position at the most likely spot for an ambush. Detecting a faint stirring he readied himself. With arched back and outstretched claws he pounced!

The end was swift.

Success!

Nancy MacLeod

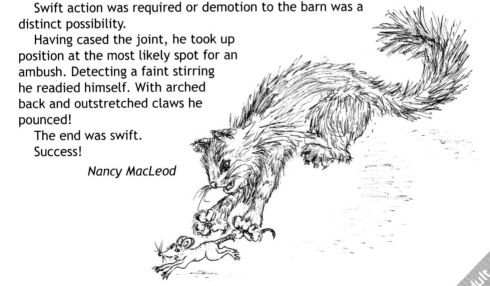

Adult

Choices

The tendon snapped — then came pain.

Sharp from the outset, but then building quickly to a level that was both obscene and intolerable. He whimpered as waves of agony pulsed through him and his vision clouded. Forced at last to cry out, his voice owed more to the animal than to anything human. His need was primordial and overwhelming.

Backing into the corner, she covered her ears and slid down, knees forming a barrier. Her face reflected the ghostly white of the snow outside but her eyes burnt with blue fire which cut any hope from his heart.

All that was left was an ending.

Mike Northeast

Chromium Steal

An unhappy woman was making the villagers' lives intolerable. She objected to everything. She needed a baby to care for.

So she drove to a distant village with the intention of stealing one. She was about to take a chubby baby from its pram when she noticed another. His skin was chromium. This is a *much* better baby, she thought.

All the way home he chattered excitedly; he wanted toys and money and freedom and in return would resent her and object to everything. She stopped the car and gawped at him in horror. The metal baby just shrugged, "Look, I didn't ask to be stolen."

Alasdair Wright

Cover Story

On a scale of One to Ten, it's a Two. The needle's scratch no worse than a bristly kiss.

"Bit of a mess," he grunts.

So true, she thinks.

"Amateur job?"

She almost smiles, remembering the compass and bottle of Quink, a conspiracy of lust and Buckfast pushing the pain below a One.

Blue entwined names scroll across her shoulder blade. Etched too deep for removal, he recommends disguise, his inky drill describing a blood clotted Japanese squiggle.

At her neck, beneath the panstick, are fingerprints in livid blue and yellow. Ice and Arnica reducing to a Seven, but she can't forget last night's Perfect Ten.

Alison Grove
Commended

Crofter Boy

The young Highlander saw Jeannie with the golden hair whose smile made life worth living.
His right hand automatically checked the pocket where he kept the ring, waiting for the moment.
The increasing shaking in his right leg jolted him back to reality.
His body was wracked with fatigue.
It was past two hours since he had heard the dreaded click under his foot.
Jeannie seemed to be reaching out to him.
The tortured muscles in his leg relaxed.
The unforgiving trigger deep in the landmine commenced its deadly sequence.
Another son of Scotland lay broken on a foreign field.
The land of his ancestors wept.

Sandy

Dear Ernest

You must be congratulated on achieving the impossible. Not only did you find just the right words, you worked within the parameters. We are not quite sure who set the task but we know that you took up the challenge. And what a marvellous outcome, so clever and thought-provoking.

Today we have been given 100 more and yet what will we achieve with that generosity of numbers? We've worked and toiled with our hearts, minds and souls and still fail to match you. So, Mr Hemingway thank you for the best short story ever written, in just six words: "For sale: baby shoes, never worn."

Paula Wild

Desperate measures

I knew she was intending to kill me. But how and when? My life became unbearable. Everyday I waited for the inevitable. Would she push me downstairs, smother me in my sleep, poison me?

One evening she cooked a mushroom omelette and I knew this was it. Two separate pans. "Here you are." She smiled but her eyes were cold. "Eat it while it's still hot."

I had to act. "Darling. There's a burnt edge to yours. Take mine." With that I swapped the plates and watched her hesitate. To decline would show her guilt. She picked up her fork and... started to eat.

I waited.

Dorothy Malone

Double Vision

On the bus to work, their eyes met — and didn't look away. They saw the world through the same eyes and were married in six months. They lived ordinary lives, never disturbing the course of history. Their lack of children caused no great regret. They had each other and that was enough.

Her cancer came as a shock but, together, they looked it square in the eye and stayed strong. On her last day, though hers were morphine dulled, their eyes still met. As hers closed for the final time, his filled with tears. It would be a grey world now, seen only through single vision.

Jane Rowe

The Dream

It was the silence that woke him: no clock's tick, no wind's whisper, an uncanny absence of sound.

He opened his eyes. The world grew stranger: no moonlight in the window, no shadows in the room, only blackness. He reached out to feel the wall, and found... no wall.

Reluctantly, slowly, he felt behind him: emptiness. Below him, no bed. Terror filled his body. His body? He brought his fingers together and felt... nothing. A mind alone in a universe of nothing.

Hours later he fell asleep. He dreamed that he lay on his bed in his room, and the moonlight cast shadows on the wall.

Jeremy Fenton
Commended

Ellen

Ellen waits by the window, her dark hair caught in a net. They have told her he is on his way and she wants to be there to see him, but she dares not catch sight of him first. What if he should be hurt, or changed, or have forgotten?

Her memory stands guard over the past but the future frightens her. She smooths her skirt down over her hips and wonders if he will know her.

The sun comes out. Outside her room, the morning crackles and blazes. She can hear the sound of his engine. She quickly draws the curtains and shuts her eyes.

Clare O'Brien Wright

The Endless War

Achtung! Achtung!
I am in charge now and you will all do exactly what I say.
No one is to move until I give the word.
You are all armed and ready to attack, but now, wait, wait.
Ah!
Here comes someone unarmed with no defence. See a spade in her hand. As soon as she puts it into the ground will be the time.
Wait, wait!
Right, attack, get her and any others you can find.
Go! Go!
Now the rain has stopped at last, it's lovely, perfect to be out here.
Oh! No! Ouch! Stop it! Go away!
These ruddy midges spoil everything.

Patricia Moon

The End Of Murdo's Croft

When the croft grid was cast over the moor, Murdo's was allocated last. Though it was largest, his was poor land no one else wanted. Still, he was young and set about its cultivation.

He scythed rushes, bought stock and incised ditches into the bog. In time, Murdo became the township's richest crofter. But as he grew old, his success was tainted by the fear that he should die with his work unachieved.

This morning, he awoke distracted and walked into the remaining wilderness at the untamed end of his croft. He kicked its profitless rock and something glinted in the sunlight. Unmistakably, it was gold.

Alasdair Wright

The Escape

It's great here at the top of the basement steps sniffing the pavement and the passers-by, especially after being indoors so long! What's that She's saying? "He's quite safe; he's too big to get through the railings now." That's an idea! Sque-e-e-eze. I'm through! Now for that bin over there! What now? Whistles! Shouts! "Fergus! Where are you? Fe-e-ergus!" But the gate's padlocked. She can't reach me! What's this? Someone's reading the phone number on my collar. He's on his mobile! Ha-ha, we're here, not in Gairloch! Now She's thanking him profusely and I'm lifted over the railings. Thanks for nothing! I'd only just started exploring.

Hilary Brown

For Dad — with love

I was a disappointment to my father. When I was six, I overheard him telling Mum, "That boy is absolutely useless!" Dad is a successful businessman, scratch golfer and got a first from Oxford.

I never did get the sporty thing and I scraped a place at what Dad called the "Mickey Mouse uni". He refused to employ me — said I'd only embarrass him.

Well, now, I'm on all the front pages. I managed twelve before they found me — not bad for a useless boy!

"Right son," the security guard snaps the handcuff on my wrist. "Let's get you safely tucked up in Broadmoor before dark."

Jane Rowe

Heart of Stone

The pebbles wet, smooth and glistening in the sunlight, recently washed by the outgoing tide, are jewels. Red, green, grey and brown speckled as the hens, to confuse the senses. They lie in threads across golden sand or in communities where the smallest, unable to withstand the weight of water gather together for company, begging to be held, touched. Drawn in by their ever peaceful state, I look to the horizon seeing only with my heart, until the salt spray, that yesterday kissed your face, brushes my cheek and my tears run to the sea. Walk your shore; caress the pebbles that yesterday were my tears.

Barbara Allen
Commended

Highland Tour

Two American couples sit finishing their breakfast in the hotel dining room overlooking the river Ness.

Soon, two cars leave the car park and head out of the town. One car takes the north road to Caithness, the other car heads to the west coast. At intervals the cars stop and cameras click.

The journey continues in a similar way until the two vehicles are again parked in the hotel car park.

Four people finish dinner, the notebook is closed, the pen put down. All the places on the itinerary have a neat tick alongside, with a brief missive at the bottom:

Highlands done!
Lowlands tomorrow!

Fiona Mackenzie

"Him"

Lying, next to him. He slept.

Breathing through her mouth, to be silent, she inched off the bed. Her heartbeat, rapid with fear, felt like it would burst from her chest.

She crept to the door painfully slowly, terror making movement almost impossible. Leaving the door open, she ran to the rucksack, hidden earlier, up the road, grabbing it gratefully, hiding now, in the safety of darkness.

Only four miles to FREEDOM!

Then, halfway, a car... She threw herself in the ditch, the headlights passed.

Concealed, near the bus stop... waiting...

The bus appeared!... a car pulled up... behind it — it was him.

P. M. Angier

In Small Time

It is the year 106 (small time) and all the very small people of the village are gathered together round the glowing matchstick and peat-crumb fire. A huge orange moon is rising in the sky amongst the sparkling stars, and all the very small people settle down to listen. Tiny frogs croak from a nearby puddle-pond, a sparrow-owl hoots and flies into a very small oak tree, and a miniscule mouse peeps out of its minute hole. Then — one of the very smallest children — who is older than you'd think — jumps up — sings a very small welcome song — and starts "Once upon a time..."

Kirsty Adam

Job Done

I stepped quietly down the ladder. Each rung gingerly felt for with relief on finding aluminium, albeit a one inch tube. This was getting harder but with costs rising and "belts having to be tightened", courtesy of the government, there was no other way. By this time, any natural light had long since departed. I edged myself down, tool bag in hand, clanging softly against the ladder with comforting regularity. Last rung and on to solid earth, when out of the darkness a hand clasped me tight on the shoulder. Caught red-handed, I was read my rights; to be held "courtesy of the government" again.

Barbara Allen

The Journey

He sat on the bench looking at the garden for the last time. Swallows performed their low-level acrobatics around him. They too would soon be leaving, their journey much longer than his. Bees wriggled their way into flower heads, filling the warm autumn air with their drowsy buzzing. He sighed contentedly, he had been happy here, not all the time, certainly not when he had been tormented by midges. As his thoughts drifted back over the past he felt a sharp pain, "Damned indigestion," he muttered. When the taxi came to collect him they thought he was asleep, but he had already gone on his journey.

R. Mapstone

Kevin and the Chicken

Kevin squeezed through the loose boards into the giant shed.

Chickens panicked, and swarmed away from him. Deftly, he caught one, gently, but firmly, pinning its wings against its body. Tenderly tucking it inside his jacket, he triumphantly escaped back outside.

"Where have *you* been?" yelled his Dad as he crept indoors.

" *Nowhere*!" shouted Kevin, racing upstairs.

His new friend stared sideways at him and blinked as he sat her on his bed.

"Stay there!" he whispered. He fetched sliced bread and a mug of water.

His sudden movements scared the hen — who squawked.

"Keep *quiet*! Then you can *stay*, and be *my pet*!"

P. M. Angier

Life's Anomalies

Why must the train be so late today of all days?

Why was I so silly having to return for my passport?

Why did I agree that when you leave for Australia if I am not there it means we are finished?

Oh Don I am coming, will just make it.

I do love you.

Hurrah, the train here at last!

Why the screech of brakes?

Why are people shouting?

What? A woman has thrown herself onto the track?

Someone is screaming and screaming.

It's me.

How could she be so selfish, so silly, doing such a mindless act, ruining others' lives?

Now mine has ended.

Patricia Moon

Like the Back of your Hand

I hold my own hand and pretend it's yours.

First, I sit on it to quiet the nerves. The anaesthetic takes thirty-eight minutes, including five for luck. Important that it doesn't wake too soon.

Then I slip my hand in mine and give myself a shy squeeze. My deadened fingers can't reply, so I work my thumb across sleeping smooth-skinned knuckles, conjuring the roughened bump of remembered calluses.

When pins and needles set in, I start up to make tea. But the kettle plummets from my drowsy grip onto my bare foot, splitting flesh and crunching bone.

Such banal agony — but it brings tears at last.

Alison Grove

Lot 106

His twin black curls quivered as he trembled on the sawdust. The auctioneer's voice boomed, barely intelligible to man, let alone beast.

Seduced by a rattling bucket he had entered the tin box. The ramp, drawn up behind him, trapped him in the dark. Then the strange sensation of lurching round corners, pitching forward and back as the rattling box sped and slowed.

Our of the dark into a cacophony of bleating and clanging and an animal reek. One small person waggled her fingers under his nose. Then he was chased out into the ring.

"Small but perfect. Come on Two Locks. Home to Gairloch."

Serena Mason

New Build

There is no door to close. Just a wide wedge of space, scaffolded, bathed in mud and builder's grit. An Teallach forges the air rolling in towards our empty windows, clouds of steam boiling from impervious stone, steel rods singing down into the sea.

I can already smell the tang of a fire burning at our bare hearth as the rain sweeps through the rafters. The boys climb ladders lashed to girders, laugh at the water which sticks their shirts to their backs.

Around our house's heart the rooms are growing shells. Inside these plotted squares we'll live. The windows wait outside, roped against the wind.

Clare O'Brien Wright

New World

Today I'm going to change the world.

I'll lace my boots and head out from the cottage along the muddy path under mighty oaks, then I'll follow the road and cut across pasture to the beach. Maybe I'll find shells of interest as I'm walking the half-moon shape of sand. I'll climb the hill then, up by the birch trees where birds sing and bumblebees hum.

Details: perhaps a toad, or roe deer caught unaware, mushrooms underfoot.

Back in the cottage I'll turn on the radio for supper music. I'll read a little, then go to bed.

The world will never be the same again.

René Grun

A Night On the Tiles

"What time do you call this? Just where have you been? You didn't even let us know you were going out, let alone ask permission. Your mum's been worried sick all night. You treat this house like a hotel you really do. Been off to see your boyfriend again I'll wager — well stay away from him, he'll just lead you into trouble. And the state of you! Dragged through a hedge backwards isn't in it. You're grounded young lady!"

I glare at her trying to see a glimmer of remorse, but in vain. She just laps at her water bowl, and her tails wags happily.

Tom Lister

The Nobody Faces

I saw it, engine shining like a black knight on a charger, sleek and smooth, hot and sweating, a smoking gun, pulling cattle trucks. I didn't imagine its arrival then, though now it seems I must; a beast of a thing, snorting, still, but only just still. Champing at the bit, a mighty grind and gone on the breath of the wind.

I saw them in the trucks, cramped and crammed in, how I felt for those faces. Men and women, children, all moving in one direction. Concentrate, concentrate you old fool, recall one, force that memory, but they passed me too fast, the nobody faces.

Barbara Allen

Nobody's Dog

I was your dog — your loyal, faithful and devoted companion. You loved and doted on me and proudly showed people my photograph. I accompanied you to work and shared your world.

Then you married and children came along and I loved them too. Later came a "career opportunity"; the family was emigrating and couldn't take a dog.

Somehow, I had gone from being your dog, to just another dog, to nobody's dog; an elderly dog in a rescue centre, unwanted, awaiting the release of the black abyss. And when the moment came, my dying thought was, "Why? What did I do to make you abandon me?"

Gillian Holt

No escape

Lucy spread the festoons of garlic around the window frames and over the door. The shadows lengthened and the sky darkened but she felt safe. This was her protection. Although the black bats whirled outside she was secure.

Remember the fireplace, Lucy.

But Lucy didn't heed this soft voice of warning.

She carried the heavy iron cross to her bed and held it close. Strange dreams made her restless. Her tossing and turning flung the cross to the floor.

The vampire bat slid down the chimney and metamorphosed into its human form. Standing over Lucy's troubled sleep he bent his head and made the mark.

Life-renewing.

Dorothy Malone

The Number

After parking his Peugeot 106 he looked at his watch: six minutes past one, lunchtime. He found a restaurant and ordered lasagne, menu item 106, and read his book while waiting: page 106, he noticed. Something niggled, but he ignored it. The bill came: nine pounds sixty and he added a tip. Outside he jumped on the 106 bus.

Only when he entered building 106 did he realise how strange the day had become. He studied the appointment card: sure enough, tenth floor, room six. Panic attacked him. He found the room. The secretary asked for personal details: name? address? *age?*

Suddenly he felt very old.

Jeremy Fenton

Only yesterday

40's night at Eventide House. The dining room was bright with bunting. Edith Turner coaxed the ill-tuned piano to deliver war year tunes. Residents danced and sang to the medleys reliving their past.

At ten Edith launched into the last song, *We'll Meet Again*. She thought of Stan. They'd never met again although she had waited. "Missing presumed dead," she had been informed.

"Some sunny day," she sang softly.

"It's not sunny, Corporal Turner, but it's been too far too long."

Edith turned. Why, it was Stan, an older Stan but definitely him.

No time for questions. Later perhaps.

"Maybe you'll walk me home, Sergeant."

Dorothy Malone

Opportune Moment

The mackerel boil was on and the sea eagle swooped, talons outstretched to snatch its prey from amongst the plummeting gannets and leaping dolphins. The fish was big and the bird lumbered clumsily into the air as its heavy prize thrashed ineffectually beneath it.

Landing on a favoured grass-topped knoll, it slit its prey open with one swipe of a claw and tore hungrily into the flesh. The noise of the waves churning on the rocks below was disguising the sounds of something closer at hand. A large animal materialised beside it and, in shock, the eagle took flight.

The otter moved in for the remains.

Shirley Powley

Out with a Bang

There were 78 steps to the top — matching his age. With meths rag in hand, he set about polishing the reflectors. Muckle Flugga's last keeper would make his exit with flair. The Lighthouse Board had it coming. How could an automated light be kept clean automatically? The b******s! He knew he was past it and was lucky to have been retained. But his days were numbered. He lit a cigarette then emptied a bottle of Lagavulin. The three-day forecast was fair — his beloved ships were safe. Turning to descend, he flicked the fag-end into an enormous box of fireworks saved for years. "Farewell Flugga!"

George Milne

The Price of Freedom

Flora was very unhappy. She had been abandoned in a cage in the garden. She had to escape. Using her powerful legs, she broke through the rusty corner and ran to the hedge. Squeezing through, she spotted two apple trees. One was green, the other red and both had windfalls beneath. She chomped as she explored the vegetable plot, the herb border and the soft fruit cage. She did not hear the shot. Her long furry ears turned bloody as the smell of cordite filled the air. The old man hung her up to drain and thought of supper — succulent rabbit pie. He was very happy.

George Milne

Miss Quigley's Percentage

Miss Quigley moved to Wester Ross to escape the rat race. She sold futures in the city but increasingly found the whole business of money repugnant. Her needs were simple, she thought; she would live on the land and grow her own food.

She bought a croft, cash, and lived comfortably off her investments while she put up the biggest polytunnel in the township.

When she took her first produce to market, however, the vegetables made it clear to her that they had grown themselves from seed and their price was theirs to keep. Although they would give Miss Quigley a small percentage for watering them.

Alasdair Wright

Rainbow

Red: my rose tinted spectacles when I met him. Orange: the channel for our tender phone calls. Yellow: the sunshine that he brought into my life. Green: the grass on the other side. Blue: his eyes as he looked lovingly into mine. Indigo: the night as we lay entwined. Violet: the deep passion of our desire.

Violet: my mood when he told me it was over. Indigo: dark thoughts of revenge. Blue: the language as we argued. Green: his wife's jealousy when she learnt of his infidelity. Yellow: his treacherous cowardice. Orange: the bitterness of vengeance. Red: the blood as his life drained away from him.

Tracy McLachlan
Commended

Reunited

She couldn't live without him, not after sixty-two years of marriage. They had never been separated. He was her crutch, her twin, her alter ego. But she had never wanted otherwise. Her life was his and his matched her own.

Without him she was nothing. She felt maimed. Abandoned.

He had proposed by Sgurr Dubh loch and had fashioned her a ring from bog myrtle. Although brittle and faded she had kept it still. Now it must leave with her.

Slowly she took herself to the loch. Slowly she walked into the cold deep waters, the ring clutched tightly in her left hand.

He'd be waiting.

Dorothy Malone

Robot

Thanks to her wonderful new Robohome all-purpose home help, Maud Worthington luxuriated in simultaneously smoking a cigarette, drinking a cup of coffee and watching a repeat of Come Dancing. The noise obscured the hum of her robotic servant as it dusted, polished, made the beds and prepared dinner.

Owing to a defect in the electronics, the machine didn't switch off when it finished the day's tasks but continued across the floor, chewing a swathe across the Persian carpet, climbed the wall, ingesting the curtains en route, crunched a chandelier on its journey across the ceiling and finally came face to face with a petrified Maud Worthington.

Mike Powley

Rough Play

Calm seas, blue skies — ideal.

"Come on, Callum — let's go fishing!"

Father and son dragged the dinghy into the water and rowed out into the bay. Callum was fascinated by the starfish and crabs he could see below, moving slowly amongst the seaweed.

A sudden splash behind then gently rocked the boat. Another, alongside, and they saw the flash of its white belly as a dolphin slid beneath them. A second fin sped straight at them then leapt out of the water in a stream of rainbow droplets. For ten glorious minutes the dolphins performed their circus act, then disappeared.

Callum's eyes sparkled. "Magic!" he shouted.

Shirley Powley

The Same Wavelength

Coffee had soaked into the note and she struggled to decipher it. It seemed to be about a debt.

What did he think he owed her? Life of course. He had been a beautiful baby but a terrible teen. Nobody could calculate what the years of nurture and the emotional investment cost, let alone put a time to it.

Usually he wrote long stories so this cryptic note was particularly perplexing.

Why did he owe her six something? There was an almost legible m. Was it six million pounds? Realisation dawned, checking the clock she clicked on the radio. His voice filled the kitchen and her heart swelled.

Serena Mason

The Seedlings

It was autumn when Marion dibbled tiny holes and planted the seeds. In the spring, vigorous young plants emerged in their hundreds, each a perfect miniature.

She lifted them carefully between rheumatic finger and an old teaspoon and eased them into pots, each one ready to fulfil a colourful new role in her garden. When all the pots were filled, there were scores of tiny seedlings left over. She was about to sweep them into the compost bin when they reminded her of something, something she had seen twenty years ago in a military cemetery in Flanders; the long rows of crosses of the lost generation.

Mike Powley

Seeing in the Dark

Shortly after my sister left in disgrace, my father planted pine saplings all around our croft house. The Inverewe foresters warned he'd planted them too close, but my father didn't listen. Then he put stock fence around the young trees — to keep the sheep out, he said.

I was too young to know my sister's crime and dared not ask, but I never saw her again.

As the pines matured, our house became darker and darker. And I grew with them until I was tall enough to see clearly in the darkness they cast.

My sister never left at all. She was under the trees.

Alasdair Wright
Commended

Seeing the Light

She woke even earlier than usual and stared forlornly at the emptiness beside her.

Beams of yellow light from the rising sun squeezed through the little gaps of her open windows. She watched them ease their way from left to right around the room, growing in intensity.

Then, she became aware of shadowy ripples reflected on the wall beside her. She thought of strings on a violin vibrating soundlessly, but listened to the lapping of the waves.

As the room lightened, the yellow beams gradually became a cold, watery white. She lay back to ponder the day ahead and realised she could now live without him.

Katy Leitch

Shoes and Gloves and Things

In spite of the biting wind Alan made his daily sortie, scouring the beach for treasure. He picked up a blue plastic glove, a couple of left-footed trainers, a deflated orange buoy and a cats-cradle of blue plastic rope entwined with seaweed, and took them back to granny's greenhouse. It was a useful haul to add to his collection and he spent the remainder of the morning sorting shoes and gloves into pairs and making coloured patterns with the remaining oddments, before standing back to admire his handiwork.

To his mind it was a far prettier display than granny's flowers, now rotting quietly on the beach.

Mike Powley

The Snowglobe

A woman walked in wastes of ice. She wrapped herself in furs and sang to raise her spirits but her breath turned to snow, and the crystals hid the beauty of the land.

Then a man came out of the mountain. His eyes were merry and although he was naked he wasn't shivering at all. The woman sang, and her snow song melted on the skin.

He slipped the pelt from her shoulders. "It's your weather," he smiled, and showed her how to sing so that the notes didn't freeze. With the warm winds came Spring rains. They walked naked in the hills, where flowers grew.

Clare O'Brien Wright
Commended

Storm Damage

The claim was for storm damage to a garage roof. We wrote to say that there had been no storm on that day. Sorry, he said, my mistake: the roof was damaged by my children who were walking on it. Fine, we said, but that is accidental damage cover which you chose not to buy. No, he said, I am claiming under the theft section of the policy for damage caused during a theft: my children were stealing my neighbour's apples at the time. Fine, but the policy requires you to notify the police of the theft. Where did you report it? The claim was withdrawn.

John Beck

The Struggle to Survive

The music thuds, limbs ache and I'm sweating. Must keep going, must concentrate. Breathing getting difficult. Water, I must get water. Can't stop, got to keep going. Fifty-five years old, why is this happening? It wasn't always like this. I am the sociable sort, love to get out of the house, do new things, meet people. Suddenly everything eases, the music stops, I can breathe. I'm out of the intense zone that took over my mind and body. People start to appear, someone gives me some water. Thank goodness, I got through it, survived, enjoyed it. And I'll be back next week for another Zumba class!

Paula Wild

Superheron

Harold Heron had been standing in stinking seaweed for two long hours hoping in vain for a tiddler to come within range of his deadly beak. Bored, his attention drifted to the blue sky, and that's when he saw the gleaming white gannet. It side-slipped with consummate ease and made a spectacular dive into the turbulent sea, reappearing in a flurry of wings and holding a fine silvery fish.

It seemed so unfair, that Harold decided to try this exciting way of fishing himself. He flew laboriously up into the sky and out to sea before peeling off like the gannet and starting his power dive...

Mike Powley

Testing The Waters

I recommend a short ferry trip from the island of Arran to Holy Island, previously called Eilean Molaise, in memory of a Christian Saint who lived there around 640AD.

Not long ago Buddhists bought this island.

A walk along the isle's West coast, leads to Molaise's cave, then his holy spring.

Further along the coastal path, worshippers have created beautiful representations of Buddha on rocks.

Buddhists remind us that our world is always in a state of impermanence.

A sign beside the spring reads

> HEALING SPRING
> Please note that this water
> does not conform to current
> EU drinking water directives.

Poor old Molaise.

Ian MacMillan

That Day

"Caitlin! Caitlin!"

Cathy was half-running, half-walking towards her, beckoning furiously. Caitlin put down her washing-basket.

"Quick! The harbour! An accident!"

"Oh, dear God — what's happened? Hamish?"

Cathy nodded breathlessly, as Caitlin rushed past her, lifting her skirts for speed.

The silent crowd gathering on the pier stood aside to let her through.

"What happened?" she shouted, wide-eyed in panic.

Kennie came to her and took her arm. Gently.

"The winch jammed. The rope broke and the end... Hamish was in the way of it... The doctor's coming..."

They carried him ashore, the rope marks livid on his neck.

"He doesn't need a doctor," she wept.

Shirley Powley

Termination at Toothache

Twitch Holloway erupted through the door of the sheriff's office and crunched the brass bell, disturbing a notice reading, "ring just once and quiet like". Seconds later the massive bulk of Swell Fullpot, sheriff of Toothache appeared, swathed in bandoliers of bullets. "Wacherwant then, Twitch?" he demanded.

"Hey, sheriff, Seven-Shot Carson's in town."

"I figured that," spat the sheriff, noting the signature mark of six neatly drilled bullet holes in Twitch's stetson.

As Twitch slumped to the floor with a low moan, the sheriff surmised the termination point of Carson's seventh bullet and rolled bow-legged out into the harsh sunshine of Toothache City to dispense justice.

Mike Powley

Withdrawal

That giant watery beast in the west, it throws thoughts into my head.

When there was the 106 story contest, that was alright. Breakers roared into evolving plot, and when I reached the rocky end of the beach the characters were talking to one another; my steps then turned into the wind and imagery lit flares.

Back home all I did was write the story down.

Now the contest is over but the stories, like the waves, keep rolling in, high tide.

Unwritten stories for a labyrinth. Hollow sounds surround. What's on the other side I just don't know.

Have another contest. Or stop the surf.

René Grun

12-17 Section

Stories are in alphabetical order of title, except the prize winners which come first.

Ciaran Alexander	RUN!
Sofie Banister	Rounded and Shiny, An Illusion? A Ghost?, Limbo
Jerome Broome	Burning a Blaze
Charlie Bulmer	The Haunted Theme Park
Kiera Clark	Daddy I'm Dead
Deborah Connop	The Road
Megan Crueize	A Silent Cry
Jasmine Easby	Time to Start Again
Charmayne Fraser	Back Away from my Thoughts
Alfie Gudgeon	The House
Patrick Hill	Star in the Darkness
Oscar Howard	Fear of the Dark
Frase Hinchliff	Canine Ponderings
Charlotte Kelman	Changing
Alexander McFedries	Why Do You Speak So Faintly?
Kenneth Mackenzie	Wilfred's Trip to the Doctor
Rosie Mackenzie	Combustion
Rowan Mackenzie	The Day I Got Thrown in the Trash
Matthew Maclean	The Best Game Ever
Holly Morrison	What If?
Ian Paul	An Intruder
Joseph Stewart	The Year 4000
Siobhan Vickerstaff	Alone at Christmas
Mairi Wyatt	Communication

FIRST PRIZE

A Silent Cry

The day of the funeral came, family and friends gathered to pay their last respects, before the coffin was silently lowered below the surface of the world. The sound of mourning and silent sobs echoed in my ears. My eyes stung as the tears welled up. Mr and Mrs Dumbfell stood, speechless and numb to everything going on around them. My heart ached at the sight of all this. Sadness overwhelmed me. People began to exit the graveyard, the Dumbfells, remaining at the side of their daughter's grave, muttered their last goodbyes, I watched silently, I wanted to call out, but I couldn't, I was dead.

Megan Crueize

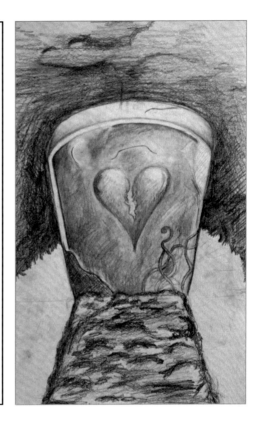

SECOND PRIZE

Rounded and Shiny

I reached down into the deep pool. The icy water nipped at the bare skin on my arm. My hand hit the bottom, it touched something rounded and smooth. I grabbed at it and lifted it out of the water. It was what looked like a small shiny stone. It was blue in colour, and marbled light and dark like the ocean itself. I rolled it around in my cold hands. It seemed to be glowing. I could hear the guns of the hunt sound. Without thinking I tossed the stone back into the waves. Maybe some things are better hidden away from man's greedy hands.

Sofie Banister

THIRD PRIZE

Canine Ponderings

I am a dog. Ruff!! Ruff!! I'm a loquacious young canine, brown in colour. My large canines help me rip and tear through the rump steak my beloved master, Winston, purchases for me.

I'm a pug, rather smug, condescending towards other dogs. They call me Doug, however my full name is Douglas Geoffrey Carlton IV. Life is pure.

I enjoy the likes of Bach, with many Picasso paintings studded around my mansion-esque kennel — original of course, I'm worth nothing less. The others, mongrels that they are, are merely jealous of me, of my silky coat, of my fine noble lineage. I am a dog. Ruff. Ruff.

Fraser Hinchliff

All I Own

Hello. My name is Eliza. Just Eliza. And that's it. That's all I own. Apart from the few pennies in my pocket. All I have is my name. Him? Yeah, that's Mark. And her? that's his new... girlfriend, Kayley. And as the waitress frowns, and the telephone rings, I wonder to myself. And as the police handcuff my hands behind my back, I sigh to myself. Would it have been different, if fate hadn't tempted me away from what is right? Would it have been different, if what is easy wouldn't have been done? Now I think about it, maybe it wouldn't be so different.

Siobhan Vickerstaff
Commended

Alone at Christmas

The door slammed shut in my face. I wasn't wanted anymore. They never loved me. Now I was sixteen they had no need to keep me any longer. It was cold outside. Snow fell thickly but silently all around me. An owl hooted from a distant tree. It took off, throwing a ghostly shadow trickling down my spine. I looked back into the little cottage. Lights shone brightly in the windows. I could see the Christmas tree. It was covered in tinsel and shiny decorations. Little red stockings hung over the mantlepiece. I sighed. I was alone at Christmas.

Sofie Banister

Back Away from my Thoughts

You'll sit for ages with a melting sweet melting in your hand, waiting for the second you're brave enough to stretch behind you and discreetly drop it on your mate's desk. The teacher hasn't looked in about three minutes. NOW!... Instant referral...

It's not just teachers that have sixth sense. It's women in general. And male teachers. I often wonder, "is my mother reading my thoughts?" Maybe she is. And then you begin to think about everything you wouldn't want her reading and your mind descends into chaos as you try to keep your cool. I don't fancy that boy and I haven't lost my new phone...

Charmayne Fraser

The Best Game Ever

One day a little boy called Robert was playing on his PlayStation3. He was playing Call of Duty. He was playing zombies, on his favourite map Ascension, and he was doing really well, until his PS3 started to smoke. He unplugged it as quickly as he could then he picked it up, but because it was so hot he dropped it on the ground. The game's console exploded and it sucked Robert inside. Little Robert was in the game. He had lots of points so he could buy any gun he wanted. He could do anything, but one problem he didn't know how to get out.

Matthew Maclean

Burning a Blaze

As the fire rages in the cinema, posters light, paper of light. The sound of screams muffled by the burning. The sweet, stenching, hoarse smell of smoke stinging my nose. As the timbers collide down hoses buzz, steam rises and fires dampen — firetrucks screech into position. Men bark their demanding orders. All that entertainment gone in one last showing. What shall happen to the cinema after the flames have left, shall it be remade or forgotten? A cigarette can create something this big, I know I'm never going to smoke. At least the popcorn will have cooked.

Jerome Broome

Changing

There she stood, tall and violet, her headwear glistening, her panther waiting and her staff shining like solid silver. I went to move forward to get closer to her... I stood on a twig. Her panther stalked towards me... then she jumped on her steed and was away in seconds. I followed her... I followed her through the tree tops... She stopped, and looked straight up at me. I did nothing but stare. She jumped up beside me with amazing elegance and said, "Tonight the banshees sing your song. You are the chosen one. You are to defeat the witches. My friend, this is your destiny!"

Charlotte Kelman
Commended

Combustion

Combustion — the process of burning, a chemical process in which substances combine with oxygen in the air and produce heat.

He did it for a living, a good living until that day when it backfired in his face, literally! The scars tell the story and they will forever more...

"The name's Jack, Jack Black, I'm here to pick it up!"

Minutes later, he walked out, dragging a big black bin bag behind. He heaved it into a red car and drove off.

Pooft! The bin bag went up in flames. He could feel it all around him, the flames spreading. I guess karma always catches up!

Rosie Mackenzie

Communication

This October, my Grandpa would have been one hundred and six — what would he have made of the Internet?

His mother acted as the local midwife, while he as messenger, travelling speedily through the inky night delivering the joyful news of a birth.

News also travelled fast when my great-grandfather averted near disaster by shouting a warning, enabling the crew of a coaster to run aground on Porthenderson Beach instead of on the treacherous rocks nearby. His powerful voice echoed across Loch Gairloch to be clearly recognised in Sand.

Grandpa could visit anywhere — without telephoning first.

Real communication: has it improved?

Mairi Wyatt

Daddy I'm Dead

My daddy killed me. He pushed me off a cliff and laughed as I fell down. He is the reason I'm evil, he's the reason that I'm coming to haunt again. I'm sorry. I didn't mean to kill the little boy. I'm sorry. Hi, I'm Ellie. I haunt people because my daddy didn't love me and killed me, my mum, and himself. He pushed my mum off a cliff and watched her fall. He killed himself but I don't know why. He beat me almost everyday and hit my mum. I couldn't do anything about it. Yes. I did kill the little boy Jack, but why?

Kiera Clark

The Day I Got Thrown in the Trash

My name is Sung. Sam Sung. This is the story about what changed my life forever. The day I was stuck in my computer. I saw a massive white hand grab me and drag me towards something that looked suspiciously like a bin.

I didn't remember getting here, I just remember a black hole appearing in my laptop and sucking me in.

Anyway this white hand dragged me up to this 2D bin and let go. I fell through a seemingly endless tunnel with documents, letters and other papers flying round me.

The next day I got a job... a job as a computer engineer.

Rowan Mackenzie

Fear of the Dark

The child walked over the threshold. His body as straight as a bow string, fists clenched. Beads of sweat caught in the vague light, glistening like stars, of which there were none. Thoughts whirled around the boy's head. What time is it? Should I be here? I don't like this. He stood there on the boundary, lonely, not affected by the cold, scared. Shadows, darting in and out of the light. Light! Light! He squinted with its brightness. The door creaked. The lock turned. The child stood, shaking with fear. There stood a tall figure, staring. It stepped into the light... "Mummy! Mummy! Help!"

Oscar Howard
Commended

The Haunted Theme Park

Mryin didn't back down. The beast came at him with razor sharp teeth. The beast was man in body, zombie in mind. Sprinting into the theme park, Mryin grabbed a metal pole, turned around and whacked the beast's gruesome head. Dropping to the ground screaming it slowly died. Smoke filled the air, Mryin looked around uneasy. He was not alone. Emerging from the choking fog came another creature, a girl, not screaming, not making any sound. Myrin gripped the metal pole ready to swing. She spoke: "I'm not going to hurt you." Dropping the pole Mryin stepped forward. She grinned with sharp teeth. "No!" Mryin screamed.

Charlie Bulmer

The House

The house was large and forbidding, Victorian and dark. It sat on the hill like a cat digesting the latest mouse, smug. When they approached it, a breeze ran through the avenue of dead trees leading up the drive, like a whispering. The garden was rambling and overgrown, with bushes poking up from the undergrowth like fists rising from the earth. When they pushed open the dark, wooden front door, an ominous creak echoed through the gloomy entrance hall. Some unidentifiable things fluttered about in the upper reaches of the roof. Then it started to rain. "OK guys, rain's coming, take five and learn your lines!"

Alfie Gudgeon
Commended

An Illusion? A Ghost?

I saw him in the distance, a mighty black stallion. As he reared he touched the sky. His hooves hit the ground in a clap of thunder. Stuck on an island with a wild stallion, I stood there in complete awe of him. He was so noble and powerful, yet so beautiful. Its mane whipped in the wind, his tail blown back between his strong hind legs. He was indeed black as ebony. For when the sun fell and the moon rose he vanished into the night. So that when the sun rose once more he was gone. An illusion? A ghost? I will never know.

Sofie Banister

An Intruder

The house was in total disarray. Drawers had been pulled right out, their contents strewn across the floor. Tables and chairs were upturned, and the television hissed with empty static, a large crack across the screen. Andrew stared in disbelief at the devastation that surrounded him.

"Hello? Is anybody there?" There was no reply. He started to climb the stairs, carefully stepping over the debris he came across. Suddenly, he heard footsteps above him. A chilling fear started to spread over him. He pressed on up the stairs, and as he rounded the turn, he saw his son.

"Found it!" he exclaimed, and Andrew looked furious.

Ian Paul

Limbo

That was my life gone in an instant. From the minute I jumped from that cliff on that cold winter's day. I suppose I didn't think before I did what I did. Of my loved ones I would be leaving behind. My mum and dad. I wish I could remember those caring, smiling faces. I can't. It seems that all happiness has been drained from my tortured, broken soul. I lost all hope when I lost you, that's why I jumped. So I could join you, but you're not there, and it's too late. I thought that by jumping I would find you. But you're gone.

Sofie Banister
Commended

The Road

It's been twenty years to the day since the accident happened. It was on this very road, this very fourteenth of November twenty years ago. She is walking, looking around every few seconds. It's dark. She is late enough as it is. She is older now. It wouldn't happen again, would it? No. Of course not.

Here it comes. faster, brighter through the darkness, it's coming straight at her. It passes. It is only a passing car. Something has her, it's wrapped around her waist. It won't let go. It's getting tighter, pulling her back. She's trying to fight it but it's too strong for her.

Deborah Connop

RUN!

Run! He told himself over and over again. Faster! They were coming. Ten zombie like things coming. Run! Right there behind him he couldn't look back or they would get him. Faster! Stop and they would get him. Run. BANG, BANG, BANG. Look ahead, a man shooting at him. Turn the next corner. No. A car coming down the road. The man with the gun right behind him as well. Get the gun. Shoot the driver. Shoot the zombies. Get in. Drive. Through the tunnel up ahead. YES! YES! YES!

Level Complete!

Ciaran Alexander

Star in the Darkness

I swung my Morning Star at the beast! I heard his bones crack as my weapon met his body... he fell and took hold of my leg to pull me over; I fell, dropping the Morning Star. I took a dagger from a sheath at my belt, stabbing his arm multiple times before it let go. I took hold of the Star and slammed it down upon this creature's skull. Blood splattered over my armour. As I sheathed my weapons I was taken hold of from behind. I struggled to get free but the creature crushed my legs. He dragged me away into the deep darkness...

Patrick Hill

Time to start again

Suddenly a flash of lightning struck Summerside farm. Rosie's house was gone. Every memory, every treasured possession destroyed, shattered into a million pieces. Luckily Rosie and her family had a shelter to sleep in until the morning but the trauma from the incident was unbearable and Rosie could not sleep. Being only seventeen years old, she felt all sorts of different emotions: sad, confused, distraught but most of all shocked. The only home she had ever lived in, ever known, was gone forever. The morning after was painful, picking up pieces of their lives, trying to put them back together. It was time to start again.

Jasmine Easby

What If?

As he sat by her bed in the hospital holding her cold lifeless hand all he could think about was their last words. The fight was just like the ones before. The shouting, crying, occasional throwing of china, but this time there was no kiss to make it all better. What did the word "sorry" even mean? A word used to make everything better. What if he hadn't brought up the coming visit to her parents' house? What if he didn't suggest she needed to get some air? Would she still be here alive, wiping his tears right now? What if?

Holly Morrison
Commended

Why Do You Speak So Faintly?

I opened the door to a dusty bar. I walked in and ran my finger along the counter, revealing a shimmering maple beneath. A large man was hunched over the bar, his hat pulled over his eyes, a bead of sweat on the end of his nose teased the barman.

I sat down at the bar and ordered a drink. The large man stirred and mumbled a few platitudes at the barman.

Within the bar, time seemed to slow down: young men shrivelled into old age, enveloped by shadows into an older world. Shivering streams of cascading light ebbed to a dull glaze coating them all.

Alexander McFedries

Wilfred's trip to the doctor

One day deep underground a worm called Wilfred went to the underground Insects' Clinic because he was suffering from blindness. In the clinic he met Barry the Beetle, Anthony the Ant and Mary the Maggot. Barry was there because he was suffering from a missing leg, Anthony was there because he was suffering from a wonky antenna and Mary was there because she was suffering from a sore stomach. Just as Wilfred was about to go to see the doctor a giant shovel came down from above and squashed Barry, Anthony and Mary. Wilfred was gruesomely cut in half.

May they all rest in pieces.

Kenneth Mackenzie
Commended

The Year 4000

Hi, my name is John. You have just found my time capsule so I will now tell you what it is like here in the future.

First of all I would like to tell you about my species. We are the most developed species on Earth. We made everything you have now on Earth like supersonic spaceships and most importantly, time travel.

We left this capsule for a lucky person to find, so you are the lucky person!

We created time travel and we can be in any year such as the beginning of time to the end of time.

So come and join us now!

Joseph Stewart

11 & Under Section

Stories are in alphabetical order of title, except the prize winners which come first.

Jasmine Brown	*The Penny Ghost*
Craig Collins	*Albert's Secret*
Megan Copland	*My Holiday*
Esther Dreisbach Pollington	*The Two Birthday Parties*
Amber Drummond	*The Shortcut*
Lily Hardy-Thomson	*Wet 'n' Wild*
Robbie James	*Little Gust of Wind*
Eilidh MacDonald	*My Dream Pony*
Emma MacDonald	*The Mermaid*
Lauren MacDonald	*What a Day!*
Mark McLean	*The New Boat*
Corey MacLennan	*The Lost Boy*
Angus Rose Bristow	*A Monster Within*
Fin Rose Bristow	*The Football Match*
Archie Snedden	*Chrissie's Cupboard Cliffhanger*
Christie Wilson	*School*
Hannah Wood	*Vampire Bite*

FIRST PRIZE

A Monster Within

" Mummy, Mummy," I screamed to mother elephant but she was entranced by death. "Don't go!" I whispered in her pancake ears. Just then three men came barging out of the undergrowth with tranquiliser guns. One man grabbed my trunk and dragged me in to the green, spiky bushes. The last I saw of mother elephant was horrible. Mother elephant had no tusks anymore! I was being dragged along the leaf covered, muddy floor and a fierce thunderstorm was brewing. My poor, fat, wrinkled legs were struggling to keep up; eventually I collapsed, knowing he'd kill me and that my end was coming close.

Angus Rose Bristow

SECOND PRIZE

The Mermaid

One day a mermaid called Shimmer was gliding through the water, when a shark blocked her path! He was very angry.

"Go away" he shouted.

"Why?" she asked.

"Because... just do" he argued. She swam away meeting a school of dolphins rushing past. The mermaid had a pet crab called Nipper but he hadn't nipped anyone. She loved riding on dolphins and racing through the waves catching a glimpse of the sky above. One day she saw a dolphin called Dancer stuck in a net. She swam back to her cave, grabbed a sharp razor shell, returned to the net and set him free!

Emma MacDonald

THIRD PRIZE

The Penny Ghost

Once there was a man. He was called Bob. He found a penny on the ground. He picked it up. He did not hear or see the shadow from behind the door of his house. It was a ghost. He was a penny ghost. A penny ghost is very greedy and this ghost wanted the coin that Bob had found. Bob walked back to his house not knowing that the ghost was hiding in the darkness. Bob stepped inside his house. The ghost pulled him into the darkness, Bob screamed, the ghost cupped his hand over his mouth and nobody ever knew what happened!

Jasmine Brown

Albert's Secret

Albert, a sixty-nine year old man, was walking back home from the pub at midnight on Halloween Night, but Albert had a deadly secret, a very deadly secret. Johnny was walking home and all of a sudden he felt something stab his neck, and then as quick as a flash he was dead! Albert's fangs dripped blood!

Two hours later Albert knocked on somebody's door... there was no answer, he walked away. A man opened the door, he saw nothing, Albert pounced out from behind a bush. The man screamed, slammed the door and ran into the kitchen, got some garlic-bread and launched it at Albert...

Craig Collins

Chrissie's Cupboard Cliffhanger

When Chrissie's mum came home she was hiding. She hated her cruel, selfish mum.

Chrissie was under the stairs under the waterproofs.

Her mum called once, twice, three times "I've a present."

"Oh boy" she muttered quietly. Chrissie loved gifts. She shuffled in the pile of waterproofs, but she stopped. Her mum had a deep man's voice and she was too selfish for presents.

Chrissie wasn't a girlie-girl. She was tough, boy-like! Bravely shuffling from the coats, she commando crawled to the door, lifting her pale hands up as a strong wind blew, but the feathers on her Aztec hat didn't move. She opened the door...

Archie Snedden
Commended

The Football Match

There was once a boy called Jack who was nine years old and loved playing for his local football team Bird FC. He loved soccer!

One morning he was getting ready for a football match against their rivals Spurs FC. In the middle of the game Spurs were winning 1-0. At full time Spurs won 1-0!

Next morning Jack had another football match. At the start Bird FC was in the lead by 2-0, if they won this game there would be a trophy. At full time Bird FC won. Jack was so glad he had been part of the triumphant team

Fin Rose Bristow

Little Gust of Wind

Little Gust of Wind was bored. He found a school. He flew in. He found some pencils and blew them away. Suddenly the bell rang. The children ran inside. "Get to work," the teacher said. "There are no pencils," the children replied. "That's right," said the teacher not paying any attention. "Hooray," shouted the children. Then Little Gust blew on the birds and made them squeak!

At break time a big boy called Chris was teasing a smaller boy called Robbie in the playground. He happened to have glasses on. Little Gust of Wind blew them away. "That'll teach him!" he said.

Robbie James
Commended

The Lost Boy

In the October holidays Jack and his family went to Glasgow on holiday. He had two missing teeth because he lost them playing football. It was raining heavily so they went shopping. Jack got bored and wandered off. He saw something he liked. When he got it, he wanted to ask his Dad if it was alright to get it. The bad thing was, there was a man wearing the same jacket as his Dad. Jack tapped the man's shoulder and the man grabbed him. The man ran away with him. Jack shouted for his dad. The man tripped on Jack's leg and banged his head.

Corey MacLennan

My Dream Pony

Once I had a dream about a pony that seemed alive and wasn't in a dream. He was shining black and I was able to jump high fences with him. He was a pony which I could ride everywhere and he seemed so real. I was able to show him to everyone and people would remember him and not laugh at me. I could enjoy him and go to shows. He was like my best friend. I could carefully groom him and tack him up. He was fast and nimble, not fat, not slow nor clumsy but sadly it was only a dream.

Eilidh MacDonald

My Holiday

I had waited for years, finally they had given in. I had wanted to take my B.f.f. on holiday with me for years.

In the airport waiting room I thought of all the years I had tried to persuade my parents and now it was really happening. My heart raced as the loudspeaker told us that our flight was nearly leaving. The trip to the plane was so exciting that I tripped myself up three times. On the plane we played we were Celebrities and pretended we were on our own plane. As we landed I thought about how Paris would be with my Best friend.

Megan Copland

The New Boat

Finally the day came to launch the boat, the new boat. She came flying down the slip. She hit the water with a mighty splash. They started up the engines and away she went, all two engines roaring away like lions. Everything was good — no leaks, no faulty engines, all fine.

Away they went, off fishing to the Minch. Sixteen hours later they were ready to fish. They put their nets down and started towing. But then they hit a stone with the net. It was stuck. They put her to full power, but it made it worse — her stern went down and filled with water.

Mark McLean
Commended

School

"But what if I don't like the food they serve?" said Gabby. Her dad, Sam, said "You love all kinds of food. You just have to find out what you like at this school."

"And what if I seem really thick to everyone else?"

"You know how smart you are," he said simply.

When they finally got to the train station she was completely out of questions. "Bye dad," she said, "see you in the summer." And he was gone in a wisp of smoke. How will I survive, she thought.

When she saw her dad after the term she had so much to tell him...

Christie Wilson

The Shortcut

Amber and Janelle were all dressed up at Halloween. "We have gone to every house in the street" said Amber. "I know but I know a house up the old road" said Janelle. It would take the girls for ever to get there. "I know a short cut" said Amber.

They had to climb up hills and jump over bogs. Suddenly, they came to a foggy graveyard. "Are you sure about this" mumbled Amber. They continued to scramble over the wall and leapt over graves. Just as Janelle was getting over the wall Amber screamed. Janelle swung round and to her horror... a bloody hand grabbed her foot.

Amber Drummond
Commended

The Two Birthday Parties

On the west coast island of Seabird, Kate woke early, really excited because today was her seventh birthday. Her parents organised a party. All her friends from the mainland were coming. It was starting at 6pm. Mum loved baking cakes but always got a bright red face from the oven. Katie went down to the shore to get out of Mum's way. She loved collecting shells and things washed up. She heard waves roaring and then thunder and lightning. Katie ran home and got ready. Nobody came. No ferry ran because of the weather. Katie ate the food and had another party once the weather improved.

Esther Dreisbach Pollington
Commended

Vampire Bite

The girl was running as fast as she could her bare feet dripping blood onto the cold, marble floor. "Jack, where are you?" she called desperately feeling her way blindly along the rough wall. "Jack," she called again, "are you OK?" Suddenly, she tripped over something lying on the floor, she fell over, landing on her hands and knees in a mound of broken glass. She said nothing, her face registered no expression, she collapsed onto her back clutching her chest.

Eventually, a boy with flame red hair, stumbled into the room. "Goodbye Beth," he whispered, and then he sunk his sharp fangs into her neck.

Hannah Wood
Commended

Wet 'n' Wild

"Cassie Estella Bell. You wake up NOW or there will be no dancing!"

Comforting words. If I wasn't practising for the Highland Floating Games I wouldn't have been late, or shouted at.

I changed quickly and then dived into the waiting car.

I arrived under scorching sunshine and then darted through the crowds to the rowing boat. I rowed over to the floating stage and the bagpipes started to blare out.

The stage was rocking violently and in a second I was in the water drowning.

I awoke on the floor of my room with the rain lashing down outside. It was just a so-called dream.

Lily Hardy-Thomson
Commended

What a Day!

Many years ago, a nine year old called Sue went to Italy with her family as a regular holiday. It was a long journey to Italy and Sue was really tired. Sue shuffled to bed when they arrived.

That night a man crept into Sue's room and took her to an abandoned house. Sue woke up very frightened. She heard noises outside. She saw it was a street and started to scream.

A stranger heard her and after breaking the door down he phoned Sue's mum. (Sue knew her mum's mobile number.) The parents came and picked her up. The family went home and didn't return.

Lauren MacDonald

106